O9-BUA-476

Ying Chang Compestine

ILLUSTRATED BY Sebastià Serra

The Runaway Wok

DUTTON CHILDREN'S BOOKS

an imprint of Penguin Group (USA) Inc.

DUTTON CHILDREN'S BOOKS • A division of Penguin Young Readers Group
Published by the Penguin Group
Penguin Group (USA) Inc., 375 Hudson Street, New York, New York 10014, U.S.A.
Penguin Group (Canada), 90 Eglinton Avenue East, Suite 700, Toronto, Ontario M4P 2Y3, Canada
(a division of Pearson Penguin Canada Inc.) • Penguin Books Ltd, 80 Strand, London WC2R 0RL, England • Penguin Ireland, 25 St Stephen's Green, Dublin 2, Ireland (a division of Penguin Books Ltd) • Penguin Group (Australia), 250 Camberwell Road, Camberwell, Victoria 3124, Australia (a division of Pearson Australia Group Pty Ltd) • Penguin Books India Pvt Ltd, 11 Community Centre, Panchsheel Park, New Delhi - 110 017, India • Penguin Group (NZ), 67 Apollo Drive, Rosedale, North Shore 0632, New Zealand (a division of Pearson New Zealand Ltd) • Penguin Books (South Africa) (Pty) Ltd, 24 Sturdee Avenue, Rosebank, Johannesburg 2196, South Africa
Penguin Books Ltd, Registered Offices: 80 Strand, London WC2R 0RL, England

Compestine, Ying Chang.
The runaway wok : a Chinese New Year tale / by Ying Chang Compestine ; illustrated by Sebastia Serra.—1st ed.
p. cm.
Summary: On Chinese New Year's Eve, a poor man who works for the richest businessman in Beijing sends his son to market to trade their last few eggs for a bag of rice, but instead he brings home an empty—but magic—wok that changes their fortunes forever.
Includes information about Chinese New Year and a recipe for fried rice.
ISBN 978-0-525-42068-2 (hardcover)
[1. Kitchen utensils—Fiction. 2. Magic—Fiction. 3. Chinese New Year—Fiction. 4. China—Fiction.] I. Serra, Sebastià, date- ill. II. Title.
PZ7.C73615Ru 2011
[E]—dc22 2010013473

Published in the United States by Dutton Children's Books,
A division of Penguin Young Readers Group, 345 Hudson Street, New York, New York 10014
www.penguin.com/youngreaders

Designed by IRENE VANDERVOORT • Manufactured in China • First Edition

2 4 6 8 10 9 7 5 3 1

To Stephanie Lurie–
the wok wouldn't sing without you!
—YCC

For my brother Carles, a great cook whose meals
always make us rejoice!
—SS

One Chinese New Year's Eve, a poor couple sent their son, Ming, to the market.

"Trade these last few eggs for a bag of rice," said Mama Zhang. "Then we can make some stir-fried rice to share with the neighbors."

"It won't be much of a celebration again this year," Poppa Zhang said with a sigh. "You'd think that by working for Mr. Li, the richest man in Beijing, we would have enough to invite everyone over for the New Year's feast."

Ming hurried off, eager to do his mother's bidding. It saddened him to see his hardworking parents being cheated by the greedy Mr. Li.

As he walked, he daydreamed about what a real feast would be like and how nice it would be to have just one new toy to share with his friends.

A small old man stopped Ming near the market. "Hello, son. I see you have some eggs there. I will trade you this wok for them."

"No," said Ming. "I need rice. Besides, your wok is rusted and has no handle."

Just then, the wok sang out:

"Boy, Boy, trade for me,
I am more than what you see!"

Ming had never heard a wok sing. He thought, *This wok is magic! If it can sing, it must be able to do other amazing things.* So he made the trade. The old man sauntered off, chuckling happily to himself.

Ming's mother wasn't happy. "Why did you trade for this battered old wok? What are we going to cook in it?"

Before Ming could answer, the wok sang out:

"Mother, make me shine so bright,

and you shall have food to share tonight."

"See, Mama?" said Ming. "It's a special wok."

"Let's do what it says," said Poppa Zhang. "We're all hungry!"

So Mama Zhang washed and polished the wok until it sparkled. Then she set it on the table.

To their surprise, it rolled off the table and out the door.

"Where are you going?" cried Mama Zhang.

"Skippity-hoppity-ho!
To the rich man's wife I go,"

sang the wok, and it briskly hopped down the road.

The wok skipped all the way to the Li kitchen. Mrs. Li was overseeing the servants prepare the New Year's feast for her family. The Lis never shared their food with anyone. The wok plopped down on the counter.

"Where did this come from?" asked Mrs. Li.

No one knew.

"Well, put it to good use," she ordered. "It will make a nice serving bowl."

So the servants put in the wok festive stir-fried rice, pork dumplings, Kung Pao chicken, steamed buns, and walnut shrimp. There was still room for more. They added long-life noodles, ginger fish, and rice cakes. Yet still there was room for more.

"Keep filling it!" commanded Mrs. Li. "I must go change for the party."

No sooner had the servants set the last bit of food in the wok than it jumped out the window.

"Skippity-hoppity-ho!
To the poor man's house I go,"

sang the wok as it trotted down the road, brimming with delicious food.

恭贺新禧

The Zhang family could hardly believe their eyes. They gleefully removed the food and set up a big feast.

As soon as it was empty, the wok rolled out to their courtyard.

"Where are you going?" cried Ming.

"Skippity-hoppity-ho!
To the rich man's son I go,"

sang the wok as it galloped away.

The wok caught up with the rich man's son, Lan, at the market, who, though he had many toys, he never shared them with other children.

The wok blocked the road in front of him.

What's this? wondered Lan. *I could use it to hold all my goodies.* And without bothering to find the owner, the chubby boy grabbed the wok.

Lan bought fireworks, toy dragons, cymbals, and drums. He piled them into the wok, and there was still room for more. So he bought lanterns, yo-yos, and kites. Finally his weak arms grew tired and he headed home.

爆竹

When Lan arrived home, he put down the wok and went to find his mother. No sooner had he turned his back than the wok hopped away.

"Skippity-hoppity-ho!
To the poor man's house I go."

It pranced all the way back to the Zhangs' house with all the goodies safe inside.

Ming bounced with joy as he emptied the wok. "There are enough toys here for all of my friends," he exclaimed.

The wok rolled over to the door and out of their courtyard once again.

"Where are you going?" called Mr. Zhang.

"Skippity-hoppity-ho!
To the rich man's house I go,"
sang the wok as it spun down the road.

The wok arrived at Mr. Li's shop just as he was counting the money he had cheated out of the poor people of Beijing. It leaped through the window and landed on the counter in front of him.

"Well, here's a nice pot to hold my money."

Mr. Li put handful after handful of gold coins into the wok, and there was still room for more. He dragged out a bag from under his counter and dumped all those coins into it, too.

No sooner had Mr. Li emptied the last of his coins into the wok than it jumped out the window.

"Skippity-hoppity-ho!
To the poor man's house I go."

It scooted down the road all the way back to the Zhangs' house with all the money safe inside.

Ming and his parents danced with delight. They invited all the poor people in Beijing to their New Year's feast. Mother Zhang served the food; Father Zhang divided the coins up among the families; and Ming handed out the toys to all the children.

In the middle of the party, without anyone noticing, the wok slid out the door.

"Skippity-hoppity-ho!
To the rich man's house I go."

It hopped to the Li house, where the father and mother and their spoiled son were weeping and wailing and blaming each other for their misfortune.

When they saw the wok, they jumped up.

"There's the wok that took all our food!" cried Mrs. Li.

"And my toys!" whined the boy.

"I'll break it for stealing our gold!" vowed Mr. Li.

The wok sang out:

"I dare you three to try and catch me!"

The Li family chased after the wok. Chubby Lan couldn't make it very far without losing his breath, and Mrs. Li had trouble running in her fancy shoes. But Mr. Li finally caught up with it. To stop the wok, he jumped inside, pressing it to the ground. "Now I've got you!" he growled.

"Wait for me!" called Mrs. Li. "I will teach that wok a lesson!"

Mr. Li tried to get up but found that he was stuck tight.

When Mrs. Li grabbed his legs to pull him out, she slipped into the wok, too!

Chubby Lan finally arrived, out of breath. “Help, help! Pull us out!” cried his parents. Lan grabbed their legs but lost his balance and fell inside with them.

"Skippity-hoppity-ho!
To far away I will go,"

sang the wok as it tumbled down the road
with the Li family inside, legs waving in the air.

Dragon dancers' drums boomed, cymbals crashed, and firecrackers banged, drowning out the Li family's cries. No one noticed as the wok sped off to the distant hills.

The Li family was never seen again in Beijing.

As for the Zhang family, they opened a shop, selling woks of all different sizes and styles. Every year, they hosted a glorious New Year's feast for all of their friends and family.

And to think that it all started with a rusted wok with no handle.

Author's Note

The Chinese lunar calendar is based on the phases of the moon. The Chinese New Year, also known as the Spring Festival, begins on the first new moon of the year and ends on the first full moon, marking a fifteen-day celebration that usually starts between mid-January and early February. It is the most significant Chinese holiday and emphasizes sharing. Many rituals and traditions are carried out. Dragon dance troupes, led by cymbal and drum players, wind through the city streets. Excited spectators light firecrackers, creating a series of deafening bangs. The racket is believed to scare off evil spirits and ensure a new year full of health, prosperity, and happiness.

Food is an important aspect of the celebration. Families and friends gather from far and near to share a New Year's Eve feast and to wish each other a prosperous and happy new year.

Among the dishes traditionally served are: whole fish and chicken, which stand for abundance; dumplings and steamed buns, representing togetherness; crab and shrimp, which symbolize prosperity; rice cakes and sweet rice pudding, symbolizing happiness; and noodles, which represent a long and happy life. The most significant dish for children is the festive stir-fried rice, cooked in a wok. The various ingredients in this dish represent harmony and happiness. Parents urge their children to eat it so that they will get along in the coming year.

The cast-iron wok was invented in China during the Han Dynasty (206 B.C.-A.D. 220). Even today, it is still the main cooking utensil used in used in Chinese cuisine. The northern-style wok, with one handle, is slightly lighter than the southern-style wok, which comes with two handles. The traditional wok is a symbol of sharing, because it is big enough to cook a meal for many families.

After reading the traditional Danish folktale *The Talking Pot,* I decided to write a story about the Chinese wok—a symbol of sharing.

Festive Stir-Fried Rice

Ask an adult to help you cook.

3 large eggs

1/2 teaspoon salt

2 finely chopped green onions

3 tablespoons olive oil [divided]

3 cloves garlic, chopped

1 1/2 cups shelled frozen green soybeans (Edamame) or green peas

1 medium yellow or red bell pepper, seeded, and chopped into 1-inch cubes

3 cups cooked rice

3 tablespoons dried cranberries or raisins

3 tablespoons soy sauce

2 teaspoons sesame oil

3 tablespoons toasted pine nuts or other nuts

1. Beat eggs, green onions, and salt in medium bowl. Heat 2 tablespoons olive oil in a nonstick wok or skillet over medium-high heat; swirl to coat pan. Add egg mixture; swirl to evenly cover bottom of pan. Cook, without stirring, for 30 to 40 seconds or until eggs are firm and brown on bottom. Turn eggs and brown other side. Cut eggs into small pieces with spatula. Remove from pan.
2. Heat remaining oil in same pan. Add garlic; stir-fry until fragrant, about 30 seconds.
3. Stir in soybeans; cook, stirring constantly, for 1 minute. Add bell pepper; cook, stirring constantly, for 1 minute. Stir in rice, dried cranberries, and soy sauce; cook, stirring constantly, until rice is heated through.
4. Return egg mixture to pan; mix well. Garnish with sesame oil and toasted nuts. SERVE HOT

MAKES 6-8 servings